Hogs Back Books
The Stables
Down Place
Hogs Back
Guildford GU3 1DE
www.hogsbackbooks.com

Printed in Singapore
ISBN: 978-1-907432-11-8
British Library Cataloguing-in-Publication Data.
A catalogue record for this book is available from the British Library.
1 3 5 4 2

For Trish Hillis

Three Silly Chickens

by

Tanya Fenton

DORA

NORA

FLORA

HOGS BACK BOOKS

There once were three chickens
whose names were Nora, Dora
and Flora. Every day they argued
about who was the most beautiful.
"Oh, what a great beauty I am!"
said Nora. "My beak is so small
and dainty."

"Not as beautiful as my soft white feathers!" boasted Dora. "Look how they shine in the sunlight."

"Nonsense,' said Flora. "I'm so tall and shapely. Surely I'm the most beautiful chicken you've ever seen?"

They argued about it all day long.

Finally, the other chickens in the hen house all shouted,
"Off with you! Go and ask the Farmer! He will decide who is the
most beautiful."
So Nora, Dora and Flora hurried off to see the Farmer, squabbling
as they went.

WAIT FOR ME ... ME FIRST ... ... ME, I SHOULD BE FIRST ... ... I'M MORE BEAUTIFUL ...

On the way, they heard a voice calling from the roadside. It was the Wise Old Goat.

"Where are you all going?" asked the Wise Old Goat.

"We're off to see the Farmer to ask him which one of us he thinks is the most beautiful," they said.

"Take care," said the Wise Old Goat. "The Farmer will like three plump chickens like you. Wouldn't it be better to be good friends, than to be arguing about who is the most beautiful?"

The goat was kind and he was sure they would come to some harm.

"Here are three wishes to help you on your way. Use them wisely as there are only three and there will be no more."

"THREE WISHES!"
said the chickens angrily.

"Who should have the three wishes?"

"That's for you to decide," said the
Wise Old Goat.

The three chickens hurried off to the farmhouse, quarrelling as they went.

"I should have the three wishes. I'm the most beautiful," said Flora.

"No, I'm far more beautiful. I should have the three wishes," snapped Nora.

"I'm much more beautiful than both of you, the wishes should be mine," squawked Dora.

"How I wish all your feathers would drop off!" screeched Flora to Dora.

In a puff of smoke, all of Dora's beautiful white feathers, which shone in the sunlight, fell to the ground.

Dora was beautiful no more.

"I wish your beak looked like a fat sausage!" shouted Dora to Nora.

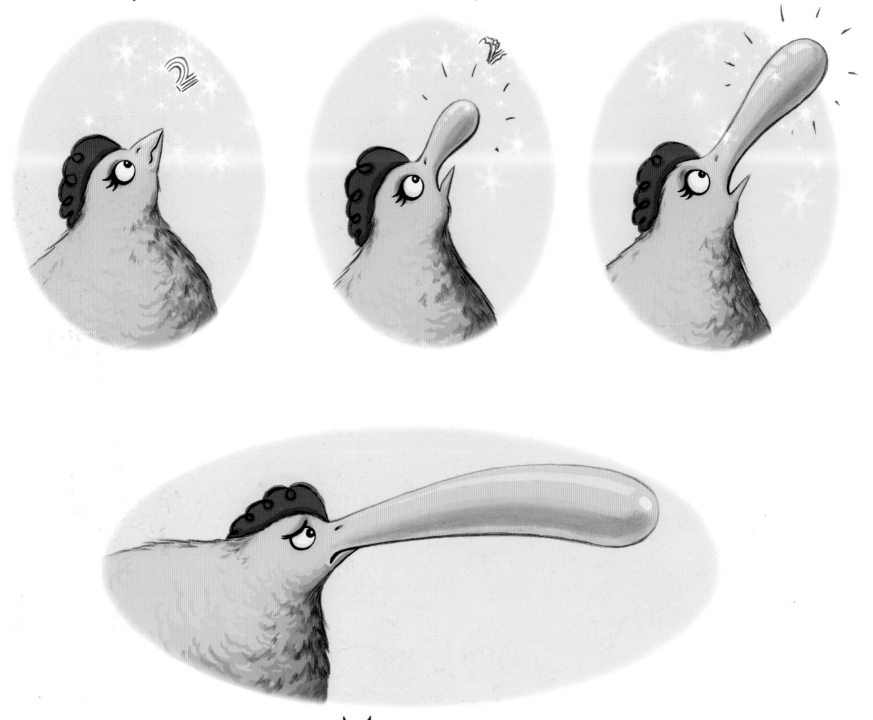

With a SQUEEZE and a POP, Nora's beak grew into a big fat sausage.

Nora was beautiful no more.

"I wish you had fat warty legs," cried Nora to Flora. With a PING and a WOBBLE, Flora's long, slender legs shrank and sprouted horrible warts.

Flora was beautiful no more.
All their three wishes had gone!

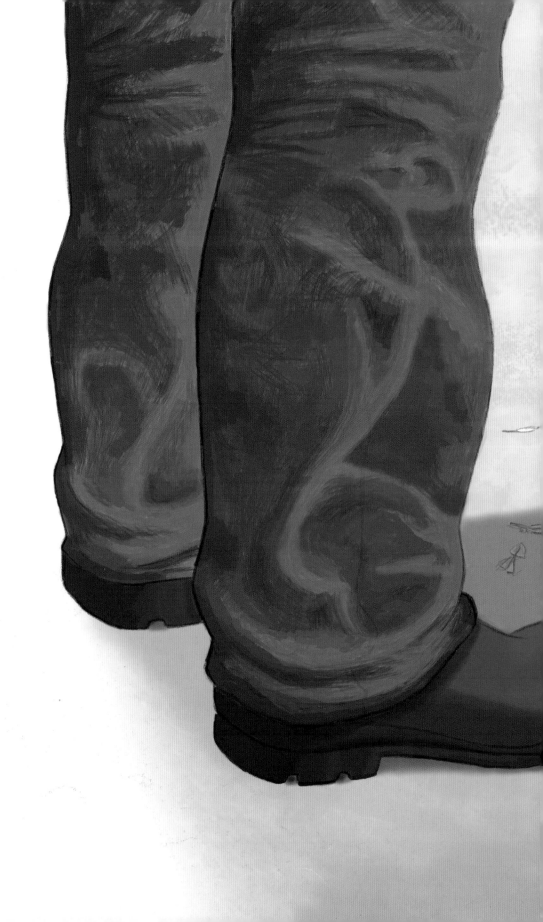

"What's all this
hullabaloo?"
bellowed the Farmer
as he opened his front
door.
He looked down to
see three of the most
peculiar-looking
birds.

"Oh, what a fright you all are!" said the Farmer.
"I wouldn't want to eat you ugly fowls! If one of you were beautiful, I would put you straight into my hot oven to cook. But you tatty lot are no good for eating. Off with you to the hen house! Go and lay some eggs for my breakfast!" said the Farmer.

They all ran off as fast as their little chicken legs could take them, back to the safety of the hen house. Never were they so happy to be so ugly. How lucky they were that they'd been saved from the hungry Farmer! They realised they'd been very silly chickens - it was much better to be good friends than to be beautiful.

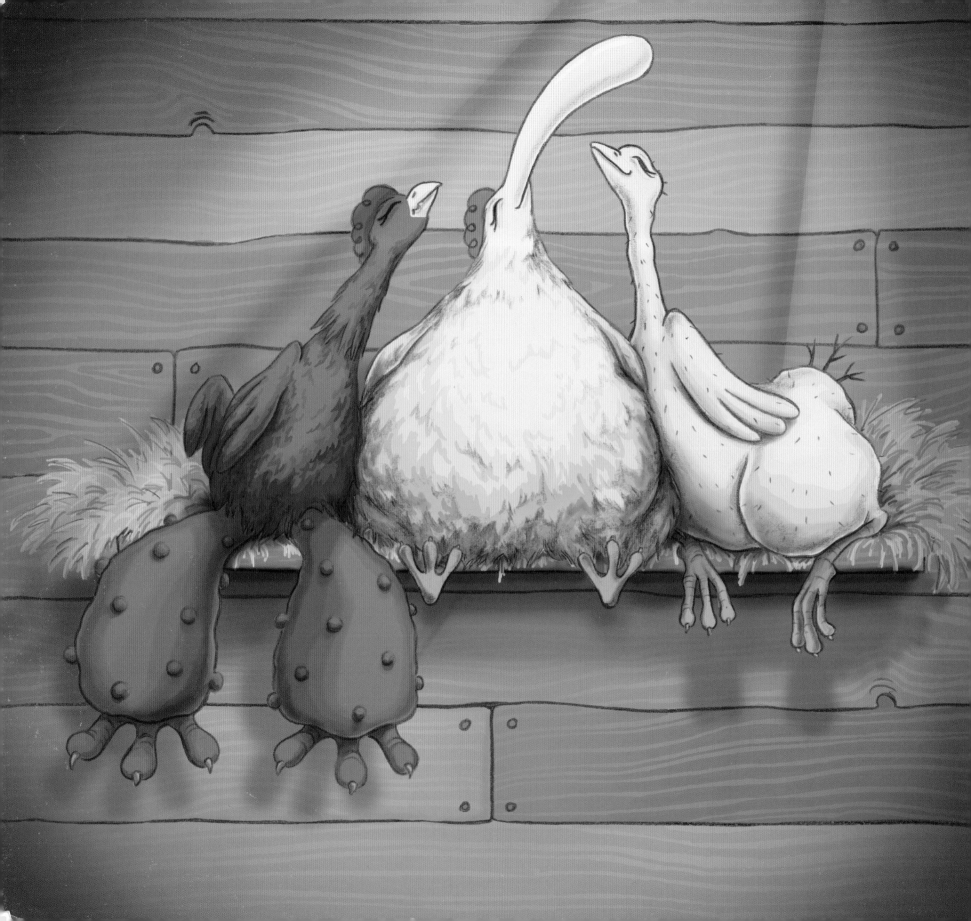

They never quarrelled again.

Until ...

The End